In the Castle

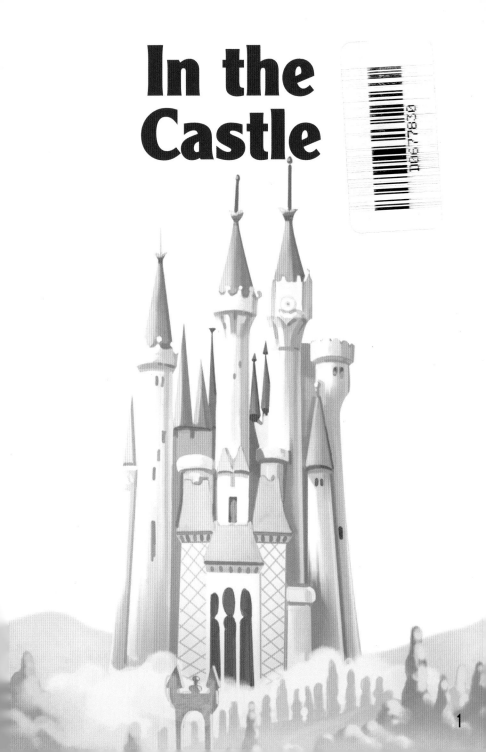

Cinderella is in the castle.
She is writing.

The king is in the castle.
He is talking.

The cook is in the castle.
He is cooking.

The musicians are in the castle.
They are playing.

Gus is in the castle.
He is jumping.

Jacques is in the castle.
He is eating.

The Prince is in the castle.
He is dancing.

Belle's
Tea Party

Belle will have a tea party.
Count what you see.

What can you count?
Here is one pink cake.

What can you count?
Here are two red roses.

What can you count?
Here are three purple plates.

9

What can you count?
Here are four white cups.

What can you count?
Here are five yellow candles.

What can you count?
Here are six good friends.